The Guest House
Death House

by

Manoj Reddy Mittapalli

Double9 BOOKS

The Guest House

Death House

by Manoj Reddy Mittapalli

ISBN: 978-93-67143-58-2

Published by

DOUBLE 9 BOOKS
2/13-B, Ansari Road
Daryaganj, New Delhi – 110002
info@double9books.com
www.double9books.com
Tel. 011-40042856

ABOUT THE AUTHOR

A few words about Manoj Reddy Mittapalli himself may help the reader to Understand his work. I am the second son of a farmer. My parents are very hard-working and deeply religious people. My Pedhamma [Father's elder brother's wife] used to tell me many stories during my childhood. Hearing all that, I was very interested in stories from my childhood. I used to study in a government school near home during my childhood. Once when I was in seventh standard, there were some competitive programs held on behalf of the government. They also had a writing competition and I participated in it and wrote a short story called 'YAMAPURI'. When I asked how you know, he said that the story Yamapuri written by you is in our school library and I have read it. I came to know that the story written sometime was recognized by the state government and published in all the school libraries without my knowledge. I immediately got home from there and went to the school where I died and looked in the library and was really happy to see that my story had been published. And so my first story was published. That day I decided that I should write stories. Due to my studies I could not spare time to write stories. But in Corona lockdown I started writing stories again.

CONTENTS

AUTHOR'S PREFACE 7

CHARACTER'S NAMES 8

I STEPS IN TO THE KOVALAM FOREST 9

II THE FIRST DREAM 12

III THE CRUEL LOVE BITES 14

IV THE SECOND DREAM 19

V CHASE THE FACTS 21

VI UNFOLD THE HIDDEN TRUTH 26

VII CATCH THE CULPRIT 33

VIII THE MYSTERY EXPLANATION 39

IX THE DEMON REVENGE 43

AUTHOR'S PREFACE

A few words about **Manoj Reddy Mittapalli** himself may help the reader to Understand his work.

I am the second son of a farmer. My parents are very hard-working and deeply religious people.

My Pedhamma [Father's elder brother's wife] used to tell me many stories during my childhood. Hearing all that, I was very interested in stories from my childhood.

I used to study in a government school near home during my childhood. Once when I was in seventh standard, there were some competitive programs held on behalf of the government. They also had a writing competition and I participated in it and wrote a short story called **'YAMAPURI'**.

After that I had to go to town for higher studies. I was on my way home for vacation, when I saw my friends, and while talking to them, one of their friends recognized my name and recognized me. When I asked how you know, he said that the story Yamapuri written by you is in our school library and I have read it.

I came to know that the story written sometime was recognized by the state government and published in all the school libraries without my knowledge. I immediately got home from there and went to the school where I died and looked in the library and was really happy to see that my story had been published.

And so my first story was published. That day I decided that I should write stories.

Due to my studies I could not spare time to write stories. But in Corona lockdown I started writing stories again. I have got an amazing opportunity to publish all my stories written through Amazon Kindle and here I present my stories to you in book form. Already my first story **ALIEN - THE FIRST STEP**, has been published in e book form.

CHARACTER'S NAMES

Vijay Kumar - Divisional Forest Officer
Srinivasan Iyengar - Wildlife Photographer
Muthu Raja - Kovalam Police [SI]
Nair - Government Hospital Doctor
Mambala, Kunjappa - Police Constables
Thangamani - Honey seller
Vishnu, Navya, Rishi, Jeeva, Sneha - friends
Aditya, Mridula - Lovers
Vignesh Varma - Nagercoil Police [DSP]
Mariappa - A villager of Kovalanki Valley
Sengaya - Kovalanki Valley village chief
Wine shop Antony - Wine shop Owner
Sulapani - Antony's first wife
Bharti - Daughter of Antony and Sulapani
Vahini - Antony's second wife
Zoya - Daughter of Antony and Vahini
Kadiresha - Merchant
Michael - Rowdysheeter
Pratap - Chennai Police [Team Member]
Rangi - Road worker
Marthanda Kurivi - The Wizard

I
STEPS IN TO THE KOVALAM FOREST

Veerinjam Light House
Coconut forest
Kovalam

One of the Veerinjam lighthouses is located on the shores of Kovalam in Kerala. Exactly 30 kilometres from there is a forest full of coconut trees. It was an area where there was no traffic, it is an area where there is darkness all around, and at least it doesn't get sunny until mid-afternoon. It was a dense forest with many animals and wild beasts. And there is a guest house in that forest area, it is a small but well- equipped place. No one lives there despite all the amenities.

Vijay Kumar, the local forest officer who noticed it, thinks that he must have occupied it. But it has been ten years since he came to that area, he will be transferred to another place. But his desire still does not die, he comes once a week and spends a good time with his companions and goes back and forth. Meanwhile, their mother's health deteriorates, so he stops going there for her treatment.

Srinivasan Iyengar is a wildlife photographer himself, comes to that forest for the very first time. After passing through all the forests of South India, he finally comes to this coconut forest in Kovalam. Although it is beautiful to look at by the sea, the coconut trees are only a short distance in front. Then everything was a dense forest. Srinivasan Iyengar came in observing all this and saw that there was a guest house there. When he goes inside, he doesn't see anyone, and that too it is not even a dilapidated house. And he likes the surrounding atmosphere very much. Srinivasan Iyengar will get the address and goes to meet Vijay Kumar. Vijay Kumar agrees that he likes the house so much that he wants it for himself and sells the guest house to him. Srinivasan Iyengar wants to change his residence to the house he has bought so much that he likes it and moves there as soon as possible.

Year: 1999.

Time: 12:51 pm,

SI Muthu Raja and his team enter by breaking the locked doors and sees a skeleton lying on the couch. It seems to be sitting there with a TV remote in its hand and a song is playing on the TV in front of it. The police turn off the TV and moved the skeleton to government hospital, and seize the house and leave from there. The same night SI Muthu Raja waits for the two constables sent to find out the details of the case related to the incident at the police station.

Meanwhile, Doctor Nair from the government hospital called and asked the SI to come immediately. In a half an hour SI arrived there.

Nair starts to say, this skeleton belongs to a girl. It is said that it has been 3 years since she died.

So, do you know the reasons behind the death? Asked SI Muthu Raja

Doctor Nair says, the exact reason cannot be said now, it needs some more time, but that the last two fingers of the left hand are missing.

Hearing all this, SI Muthu Raja leaves from there to the police station and on the way he has many doubts.

Who is that girl?

Who killed her?

What happened to her two fingers?

What was she doing in that house?

How does TV run if she's been dead for 3 years?

Did the skeleton move here from somewhere? Or

Is that TV on air for these 3 years?

If this is true then how is it possible for 3 years?

He reaches the police station amid many doubts. When he went inside, the two constables he had sent to find out the details were lying dead. Seeing that, the SI Muthu Raja is shocked and searches around but no one is there and immediately calls the CI and tells what happened and immediately takes them to the hospital and registers a case.

In the morning they go for him who told the police about that guest house. Ask him for details and he starts telling what he saw.

Exactly one month ago,

I earn money by selling honey in the forest and one day went towards that guest house on a bicycle with the honey I have taken. Seeing the house from a distance, I had noticed the sound of some songs coming from inside. Thinking that some madman is living in this guest house in such a thick forest, ten days later, when I was walking on the same road again, I heard the same songs from that house again and I ignored it. This time, due to good demand we have to go the same way again to collect honey. As my brother hears the sounds of the same song again and again, he told let's go there and see. But while thinking why we are going away from that idea, it starts raining.

We were there under the tree and as the rain was getting heavier, he decided to go near the house. We take the honey bottles and reaches home with our bicycles. There, hiding our heads in front of the house, my brother noticed the same song repeating itself. In the dense forest, the sound of that song in the midst of the fierce raindrops is what motivates him the most. He looked at the door crookedly to see who the madman is listening to the same song over and over again, but it was in closed. He goes closer and knocks on the door but no one opens it so he pushes hard but realizes it is locked.

He turns around thinking that there is no one in the house as he doesn't even see the shoes outside, and then he turns back and tries to look inside through the hole of the door latch, suspecting how the song will be heard from inside. But it was all moldy, so he took a small stick under it, put it in it, turned it around cleaned it, blew it well. And when he looked inside, he saw that the song was playing directly on the TV. Looking around at the TV, something thin and white is seen directly to it. While wiping his eyes well to see properly and looking inside again with more interest, we see something like a skeleton in the shape of a man from that small latch hole, suddenly with a terrible sound, some shape appears in front of his eyes. Get scared and falls back down on the ground, gets up and runs away from there.

II
THE FIRST DREAM

Time 1:32 am
16th November 2022
3B, Manyasri Apartments
Amaravati, Andhra Pradesh

Vishnu wakes up from sleep and looks around in fear. Meanwhile, he hears a voice from the dark room.

Shhhhh..... If you say You will die!

Who are you? He shouts. But there is no sound, no one else. If he takes his phone, it is not charging and if he puts it down, there is no electricity. A little scared, he opens the door of the bedroom and there is an electricity in the whole house, but Vishnu notices that electricity is not in his room only and when he thinks to go to his friend, he hears the same voice again.

Shhhhh..... If you say You will die!

He starts to hit the door of his friend's room, but he does not open the door. While Vishnu was still hitting, suddenly something pulled him into his room and closed the door. Vishnu was shouting loudly, Heard the same voice again. And his shouting stopped.

Back to 1999

Day after Police Murders,

After hearing what the honey seller said, SI Muthuraja goes to his station. After that, no matter how much investigation is done with his team, it is not going forward. Despite trying in various ways, the person in the house and who killed the two constables was not known why they were killed, and no evidence was found. So the case was pushed into unsolved cases forever. After some years the person who sells that honey also dies. As he was the person who saw that, and he died in that too, some people remember it, but others dismiss it as a myth. Eventually, everyone there will slowly forget the incident. In a few years, all the policemen there will be transferred and go to other areas.

"Days turned into months, months turned into years."

All around, Kovalam is very developed for tourism. Boats were moored in that sea area, many shops, guest houses and hotels were established around the lighthouse. Reminiscing about the old days is a rare task as the world advances in technology as well as in the ever-increasing population.

But no matter what happens, no matter how much it changes, the forest remains the same.

III
THE CRUEL LOVE BITES

Year 2017
Gurbhani Cafe
Hyderabad, Telangana

Aditya, who is very cynical in the office, goes to the nearby cafeteria for some relief. He ordered coffee and put it in front of his laptop and was busy doing his work. Meanwhile, a small ripple didn't seem like it was actually bothering him, but he couldn't help but roll his eyes. Just then, Aditya sees for the first time 'Mridula', who is stepping inside with his friends, smiling as beautiful as a blooming jasmine flower, as if all the drops of sandalwood have come to the surface of the earth. Strangely, they sat facing each other in a coffee shop like a married couple. Excitement and mischief are slowly pervading the air. The soft sound of a piano with the fingers of a talented musician fills the cafe beautifully. The soft cheeks of those who are listening attentively to those sounds shine with happiness. Aditya sees her face light up, completely enthralled by her passion for music. Aditya can't help but admire the real charm of the girl especially how her eyes dance to every note played. Aditya's voice was full of longing as he was close to him.

Tell me what is the song that touches your heart? Asks Aditya.

His mind was eager to know something about the girl's passion. After a moment's pause at Aditya's question, a smile graced her lips. Instead, she leaves without telling so. Gets frustrated that he could not find out the girl's name at least and leaves from there.

After a week,

Aditya goes to the theatre to watch a new movie as it is actually Sunday. While the movie is going on, someone comes and sits in the front row. He doesn't care much. In the darkness of the movie, he sees the shining ear rings hanging on the cheeks. While trying to talk to her that there is no point in leaving this girl, the girl goes away from there, and immediately he also follows her and reaches the lake under the nearby cable bridge.

The girl disappears from his sight when the population is a bit high, as a tourist area surrounds the lake. He is feeling all the pain of missing again, and he sees a kite flying in the air. Aditya who is watching it sees the girl behind a little boy who is pulling the kite, and he flies in the air with happiness. In front of him, there was a distance that the girl couldn't reach. There was a small thin water channel in the middle and on the other side of it, the girl was on this side.

Amidst many efforts, the girl accidentally sees Aditya and immediately remembers him. A shy smile played on her lips.

Aditya raised his hand and softly said "Hey"

His voice was transformed into a word by the water above the canal and carried gently to the other side. The girl's eyes glowed hazel in the dim light.

Soon the girl also replied "Hey"

And her own smile started to reflect him in the flowing water. As the sun sinks below the horizon, casting a warm light over the great city, Aditya approaches the girl slowly, channelling some unknown feeling to conquer this world. She stood there on the edge of the lake, her bare feet sunk into the cold sand, her hands engaged in mending the falls of the hairs, her intoxicated eyes piercing him like needles.

Aditya takes a step closer to her as the heat radiates from his body. The girl stared at him, her heart pounding in his chest. It's like a language of emotions talking to each other internally in a way that at least words can't.

While there is a terrible chaos around, there is a quiet world between the two of them, breaking the silence, a word from him saying may I know your name?

His voice breaks the door in front of the girl's ears and enters. To which the girl replies 'Mridula' with lips softer than mercury, sweeter than honey.

Perhaps the feelings of both of them were mixed together, and like a bit of love, they became even closer and started life in a new direction. Since then, they both like a cup of coffee in a cafe, like a movie audience in a theatres, like couples on benches in parks, like worshiping God in a temple, like walking in the streets in the evening. They also like shopping in malls on weekends, like a long drive to new places during vacation sometimes they like sitting with friends, like going for a walk. It goes like a lovely riot. The love between the two is also growing. All this is known in the house of the soft ones for some years now, it is time to face the challenges. Mridula's parents have a lot of speculations on her and her career, so they don't agree to their love.

No matter how hard they tried, their stubborn attitude remained the same, and they had to decide whether they wanted love or a future. So Mridula decides that she wants love and a loved one and comes out of that house. While the two are in the process of tying the knot for their new life together, Aditya has to go to Thiruvananthapuram for office work, so Mridula says that she will also come. On the first day of his visit, Aditya finished his office work and went to all the nearby places to see the outside world of Kerala. Then they hear about an area called Kovalam, which is exactly 20.5 kilometres from Thiruvananthapuram. There is a lighthouse beach there, it is very good, and recently it is in the front line of tourist places, and they decide to go there.

They get up early the next morning and leave to go there. As the omen was, the clouds were thick and black even in the early morning, don't know what happened, but the sun stopped rising in the sky. However, when they both book a cab and reach the lighthouse beach, they see how the sea coast area looks like their looks are stuck in the clouds. The sea is flying to the shore, and it looks fierce in black and blue combination. They're wanted to go back, but both thought however we came to here, let's stop for a while.

While both were walking along the seashore, it started to drizzle for a while. As the area has already developed so well, hotels and resorts have been established in front of the coconut forest near the coast. While the two reached there together and looked at the surroundings, it was interesting to see the dense forest behind them and the raindrops falling from the middle of the trees in the little light. While the two were walking inside little by little, the drizzle turned into rain and those who had already gone inside stood under the big trees nearby.

If they are coming to go back somehow, they will forget the way they came in the middle and go on another way, they cannot see their destination. Just then they both see that lonely house in the forest. They reach that house saying that there is some house, let's hide our heads there for a while and leave after the rain subsides.

In the darkness of the rain, they don't know the time, and it doesn't even stop, and since the evening is over, they think, let's go inside the house. Even though the doors are not that strong, they open when pushed a little hard.

The stale air fills their lungs, and they look into the darkness beyond and take out their phones and turn on the torchlight. The interior is in the same place as it is, but it looks a bit dilapidated, and as he moves forward, while inspecting each item closely, a book falls down from the shelf.

Their hearts and anticipations pounding with fear, they take their first steps into the room with a deep breath. Dust- covered cobwebs from an old chandelier hanging above decorate the interior giving it an eerie look.

Their eyes widened as they looked at the strange objects scattered around. Files of ancient books lined the walls, their leather covers worn and faded as their curiosity got the better of them, and they were deeply drawn to the houses.

Meanwhile, the storm roared like a furious beast, its deafening claps echoing through the night, the wind constantly shrieking and dashing against the windows with tree-splitting force.

The fury of the storm can be heard in the deafening roar of thunder, as lightning briefly lights up the night sky. Fierce winds and clouds roll in, making the storm seem as if it has taken on a life of its own.

Herds of wild beasts howl like banshees, the deafening howl of the storm thunders, and the angry howls of the wind try to tear the foundations of the house, and the heart of the gentle beats with fear. Soft hands were tight and tight as she held them together, the wind whipping her hair as her knuckles turned white from the strain. Immediately, Aditya was held tightly like a skunk in fear.

The violent situation subsided little by little for a long time, the storm retreated to the house of clouds for rest, the wind hid in the trees, and the silence of the forest seemed even more frightening.

Mridula feels that everything is very bad and asks Aditya to leave here, but now it is very dark, he says let's leave at dawn, we have to stay here tonight, we have no other option. The charging of the phones near them is also decreasing. One side is hunger and the other side is darkness.

There is a forest in which there is a house in it. Even though it is a little difficult to imagine, they must be there, but if they turn on the light, it does not seem to bring them back to life. As the surrounding cold pierces both of them like needles, they touch each other beyond the limits to infuse heat into their bodies.

Each other's hands were clasping each other in a warm hug, the heat was already starting to ignite a little fire in both of them, but it didn't take long for the fire to burst into flames. As shivering lips are fuelled by sweetness, both of them become naked in the fiery flames. While enjoying that moment, there is a small disturbing sound in the house, but they are not on the verge to care about that sound.

"Warnings are always small because the dangers that follows is so, so violent".

In the lights of the phones, a shadowy figure appeared from the corner of the door of a room next to the hall. Mridula showed to the Aditya. He slightly bend and trying to see what is in inside the room then suddenly that shadow drag him in to the room shouting with the wild voice.

IV
THE SECOND DREAM

Time: 3:54 AM
16 November 2022
Manyasri Apartments
Amaravathi, Andhra Pradesh

Navya suddenly opens her eyes and gets a little scared, seeing that it is 3:54 in the night. The sound of ticking...tick...tick on the wall clock in front of her was painful in the room, like her heartbeat. Meanwhile, an unknown voice is heard from somewhere.

Shhhhh..... If you say........ You will die!

Out of fear she calls Vishnu, but it doesn't work, she calls another friend, but it also doesn't work because there is no network signal. While the voice is recording everything that has happened, again the same voice is heard.

Shhhhh..... If you say........ You will die!

Navya's heart raced at the speed of light amid the echoing sound of that clock in the quiet room, quickly recording the voice. This time the same voice is heard for the last time, Navaya's finger leaves the top of the record button.

Back to 2017

The day after the storm,

The next day after the terrible situation, the forest conservatorship officials send a team with some forest conservators to find out whether there has been any damage to the forest due to the intensity of the storm and whether there has been any loss of life of animals.

As they went back and recorded the loss of animals and plants, as it was about noon, they all reached the abandoned house for lunch and thought that they would rest for a while and then leave.

A member of the group looks around the house and goes inside, where he sees a girl lying naked and dead and immediately calls everyone.

Everyone reaches there and is surprised to see a dead body of a girl naked in the forest and calls the authorities.

They see two phones next to each other, both are switched off. Bodies will be sent to the government hospital for postmortem, a case will be registered and the girl's parents will be informed based on those two phones. After collecting details from them, the police confirm that the second phone belongs to a man named Aditya, who left from the house with her in love and to get marry.

But as the dead body of Mridula was found there, an FIR was filed that it was Aditya who killed the girl and ran away.

After post-mortem, the dead body is handed over to their parents for last rites.

Surrounding people are started to spread the news that exactly twenty years ago, a girl's skeleton was found in the same house, and now another girl's body is found in the same house.

Within a few days, that guest house becomes a death house.

V
CHASE THE FACTS

Time: 6:47 AM
17 November 2022
#10, Shiloh Cottage
Hyderabad, Telangana

Mother stopped the alarm that was ringing so loudly that 'Jeeva' would wake up from sleep, scolded Jeeva for still sleeping well even on the festival day, put coffee in his hand and told him to come downstairs to freshen up quickly. After a long time he came down while bringing breakfast to him with love, and he got a phone call saying that your friend has died. Jeeva picks up 'Sneha' on the way to leave and reaches the hospital. When the police reached there and collected the details, they both went there.

The both friends are asked by the police, is he your friend?

They said "yes sir".

And this girl? Police again asked them.

Both are not understood his question and doubtfully asks him which girl, sir?

Police moved a little sideways, and said this dead girl?

By seeing that, both of them are shocked because there is not one but two of their friends who are dead, they are Vishnu and Navya. Jeeva Sneha is drowning in grief and both confirms that girl is also our friend. When they asked the police how they died, they told them that we got a phone call in the morning.

The milkman used to put milk packets for everyone in the flats early in the morning. He is doing the same today. He saw that the door was slightly open. When he opened the bedroom door, he found Vishnu dead and called us. When we searched the whole house, we saw that there was another bedroom next to it, and when we opened the door, we found this girl dead there too. When I asked the milkman, he said that these two are your friends, that's why I called you, and when the policeman inquired about them, Jeeva started saying that this is what happened.

We went on a tour together with five friends. On the last day, we went trekking to a forest in an area called Kovalam. We left again as soon as to catch the train, and we reached whose houses at midnight, but we did not know that these two were in that same house last night.

Both of them dead bodies are handed over to their parents. Grieving relatives, parents between tears. After completing all the ritual programs in the evening, while going back Jeeva received a sound from WhatsApp, it was a voice recorder from Navya. Immediately they start listening to it, Navya tells about it that I had a dream, and I open my eyes heard a voice that someone will kill me here, who is not visible, I am very scared.

Meanwhile, they both are also heard a voice from voice recorder. Hearing that Jeeva and Sneha both become silent at once, they look at each other with fear in their eyes but both of them do not open their mouths to speak a single word. Because they both know that the dream came not only to Navya but also to them, they know that the voice is not a dream, and it is true. They know that if they say it, it will kill them too.

Because the day before that trek they went to the guest house in that forest, they all went to different sides. While looking at the house, Sneha saw something above the sofa and called Jeeva and found it written on the wall.

Shhhhh..... If you say........ You will die!

Jeeva gets a call from the police, when he picked up the phone, the police asked him only one question...

"Five people went to trekking, two died, two came to hospital, and where is the remaining one?"

Immediately they make a call to 'Rishi', but his phone doesn't work, they keep trying again and again but with no result they call to his mother.

Rishi has not been seen since morning, and he was there last night, but he is not there since morning. I don't know where he has gone, I tried all kinds of things, and even I couldn't, I told my brother, he has already left and will be here soon, Rishi's mother says.

Knowing all this, both Jeeva and Sneha are heartbroken with fear.

Did Rishi also get the dream they got?

Did Rishi also die like Vishnu and Navya?

If alive, where is he? They are concerned with various doubts.

The next morning,

'Vignesh Varma' reaches Rishi's house in Velachheri in Chennai along with his family. He is the younger brother of Rishi's mother. Vignesh Varma has been an active man since childhood and chose such an active career. He got the post of DSP of a town called Nagercoil in Kanyakumari district and used to perform police duties there. When his sister calls and tells about the matter, he leaves immediately and reaches

Chennai early in the morning. As soon as he arrives, he is bombarded with all kinds of questions, and immediately begins the investigation by telling the two friends to come to Chennai. He learns everything that happened since the five friends went to Kovalam. When checking the CCTV cameras in front of the house, there is a record of Rishi coming to the balcony outside the house the night before, looking at the wind here and there scared and leaving somewhere.

The police search the entire city of Chennai day and night, but they do not find any trace of them, they advertise in the newspapers. Meanwhile, Jeeva has a suspicion that if Rishi has gone to Kovalam. After knowing that, Vignesh Varma spoke to his superiors and formed a team and reached Kovalam with the help of Kerala Police. Approaching the guest house in the coconut forest, one observes the surroundings. Dense forest, dilapidated guest house, it's a scary place to look at.

While going back to the police station from there, a village called Kovalanki Loya is seen in the middle. It was a barbaric village with ancient superstitions still undeveloped. The policeman stops a man and asks about the guest house in the forest, 'Mariappa' tells him that it is a cursed place and anyone who goes there alone or touches the things there will die.

They considered that it is a superstition, Vignesh Varma reaches the police station from there and starts examining the files of all kinds of suspicious deaths around the guest house. Once in 2017 two lovers came there and then the girl named Mridula had killed by her lover Aditya, and he ran away. Vignesh Varma called the SI and asked about it, and they said that they closed the case as he was not found no matter how much they searched.

What is the evidence that Aditya did the murder?

Aditya might also be dead, right? Vignesh Varma shout on policeman that why you didn't investigate like this way.

From the next day, even in Kerala, Rishi will be advertised in newspapers.

Vignesh Varma divides the police into two teams and sends one team to find Rishi, while the other team is taken along with him to reopen the Mridula case and investigate. Jeeva and Sneha, who came with them, are told to stay there in the office. The two of them were walking from the office thinking that they should stay there all day and feel tired and go out. As it was the snow season, even at 9 o'clock in the morning, the hills were covered with snow like a blanket, while the trees swayed slowly in the midst of the mist, each drop of water from them turned into droplets and fell down. Now and then the thin rays of the sun penetrate between the leaves and reflect on the drops of water, making the entire road glitter like pearls along with the grains of sand which are invisible to the eyes above the road below. Jeeva and Sneha pass all of them and reach the village of Kovalanki Loya.

It was a small village, huts all over the village, maybe 30 in all, it was a village mixed with old-time people with snow bushes and hut attics. As they enter the village, everyone looks at them strangely, and then Mariappa, whom they met on the way the day before, appears.

Immediately go to him and told about the dead people by saying that "we went to that guest house where you told us yesterday. Now we are looking for our friend Rishi", who is missed.

After knowing everything, Mariappa takes them to the village chief 'Sengaya' saying that if you want to know all the truth about that guest house, you have to meet him.

It was a hut in a corner of the village, and as soon as both went there, the weather changed so much that the coldness that had been there till then made them sweat a little. All around the hut there are lots of fire, thousands of threads for each stake, and some statues inside, it looks like a strange place to look at.

In the meantime, Vignesh Varma called and asked where they are.

Jeeva forgot to hang up the phone call, saying that "we are near and coming". Jeeva, Sneha and, the person who were on the phone call, heard a loud voice saying that

"Stop there."

Coming out from within the hut - Why are you going back?

Don't you want to know what happened? Says Sengaya.

Those both friends who heard his words lost their fear and became anxious.

How do you know us?

Why did our friends die?

What happened to those in the guest house?

Jeeva asks him, and Sengaya starts telling about the guest house and the people who once lived there.

VI
UNFOLD THE HIDDEN TRUTH

A few years ago
Kottaram Village
Kollam District, Kerala

A man named Wine shop Antony used to earn his living by running a small wine shop in that village. He had two wives named Sulapani and Vahini. But the first wife Sulapani, lost her womb some years after the birth of her daughter. Wine shop Antony was forced to remarry Vahini for his heir due to pressure from his father. But the second wife Vahini also gave birth to a daughter, the first wife Sulapani started hating both of them. He married someone else for a son because I had a daughter, but even though, she was happy that Vahini also had a daughter. She was jealous that Wine shop Antony was spending most of his time with his second wife. Sulapani had the mind-set of wanting everything for myself, giving everything to myself, caring only for me, giving importance only to me.

After some years, the wine shop, which was run by Wine shop Antony, caught fire and burned down. Since then, the family's finances have deteriorated, and it becomes difficult to even eat a single meal. At the same time, Sulapani and Wine shop Antony had frequent quarrels.

Wine shop Antony spends most of his time with his second wife Vahini for peace. As Sulapani does not like all this, continues to argue that we should go to another town and have a separate living, Wine shop Antony gets angry and beats his wife in a drunken state and goes to Vahini to sleep with her that night.

That day at midnight the whole village was quiet and everyone in the house was fast asleep and Sulapani woke up. She slowly takes the little money in the house and brings a bag of clothes wrapped in the evening, and wake-up her daughter 'Bharti'. While escaping from that house, she sees her husband sleeping with Vahini. As hatred danced in Sulapani's eyes, she took a can of kerosene from the side and poured it all over the house and burnt everyone in their sleep. No one in this world could have had the joy in Sulapani's eyes standing outside watching the house burning in the smoky darkness at midnight. Without even a minute's delay, she immediately took Bharti from there and left the town overnight.

So, after a long journey of three days, both mother and daughter reach a small town. Sulapani's eyes were full of fear as there was no one to help them in that town. Taking her daughter and walking in the streets, suddenly she sees money in front of her eyes.

"Finding money is not wrong, but where it is found is wrong".

Opposite her, a 40-year-old woman was instantly attracted by the money in her hand. Seeing Sulapani looking hopeful, she said only one thing.

"If you want money, you have to work hard, but that hard work should not give sweat like everyone else, but it should give physical happiness.

If you think that your body is not yours for a few days in your life, your daughter will make a gold crown over her body for the rest of her life.

Hearing all this, "the roots of the tree of desires are firmly planted in Sulapani's mind, and the lines of the old life form are completely washed away in her imagination".

The kind of life Sulapani wanted was exactly what she wanted, and she went after it without a second thought. Sulapani, who left her daughter outside the house and went inside with her, came out after a long time with a handful of money. Sulapani's face is lit up with happiness. The hope of wanting more made her go inside the house again and again. With the money she got, she rented a small house nearby and used to go to that work every day from there.

While things are going well for a few days, if the owner of the house where Sulapani is staying is not feeling well, her son will come and take care of her. Only then does Sulapani know that her son is a forest officer, whose name is Vijay Kumar.

Vijay Kumar, who is not even married, can't help but be attracted to Sulapani, who lives in a rented house, even though she has an 18-year-old daughter, who walks around in front of his eyes. Soolapani also provokes Vijay Kumar to show off all her beauty and motivates him more. After a few days, when Vijay Kumar's mother's illness worsened, as per the doctor's advice, she should be confined to bed, and she should be accompanied by a man at night, he prescribed some medicines and left.

Sulapani, who has been waiting for an opportunity for many years, is happy in her heart that the opportunity has come to her because of her mother's illness and makes all kinds of helpings. One evening, Sulapani cooks a good meal for Vijay Kumar and takes it downstairs. She tells him to eat as much as she has brought it for him and touches him physically on the same pretence, saying romantic words and takes out all the inner desires and puts them in his mind. Soolapani asks her daughter Bharti to look after Vijayakumar's mother that night and invites him to come upstairs. She served the feast of desires in her on the bed of sexy flowers and satiated the hunger of lust in him and showed him heavenly abode all that night.

Since then, the illicit relationship with him has been endless. Even though she had a grown up daughter at home, doing such things took away everything that still kept him in delusion. He spent all the money on her, kept everyone away and made Sulapani his world.

Finally, he gave that house also in the name of Sulapani. Sulapani, who thought her work was done, threw Vijayakumar out of the house.

She said that "the house is mine, and I don't know who you are".

Moreover, she started prostitution in the same house. Sulapani not only engaged in prostitution but also brought some young women from other areas to engage in prostitution. Gradually she targeted the big businessmen and the wealthy. She used to put in honey trap and have illicit relations. Having a luxurious life, she eventually forced her younger daughter, who was staying at home, into prostitution. Sulapani has accumulated assets of lakhs of rupees. It has become a habit of honey trapping the big boys, grabbing all their properties, doing something and keeping them away.

In the same order, 'Kadiresha' was introduced to Sulapani for a few days. Knowing that he is a well-to-do man who has earned lakhs of rupees from businesses, Sulapani thinks of a golden chance. Kadiresha was caught in her net and extorted thousands of rupees, Kadiresha gave most of the money earned to Sulapani. He also ran out of money and started going into debt. Knowing that he had nothing more, Sulapani slowly pushed him away.

One day while going to Sulapani, Kadiresha for the first time saw Sulapani's daughter Bharti. When he asked, that he wants to sleep with her daughter.

Sulapani says that "my daughter is not like that".

Several times, Kadiresa brutally harassed Bharti, and a disgusted Sulapani wanted to get rid of his torment. Waiting for a good opportunity.

Meanwhile, as Vijayakumar's mother is getting sicker, and he has no money to treat her, he learns that Sulapani has also forced her daughter Bharti into that profession. Thinking that it is a good moment, he slowly approaches her daughter by saying magical words. He used to take Bharti to his guest house in the Kovalam forests once a week without Sulapani knowing that. He used to take money from Bharti and give the necessary treatment to their mother. But unless the doctor does an operation on her, there is no chance of her health getting better with these medicines. So he needs a huge amount of money. Just then, wildlife photographer Srinivasan Iyengar comes looking for Vijayakumar.

Srinivasan Iyengar says, "I like that house so much, I will buy that house and give you whatever money you want for it". By listening all that, Vijay Kumar jumps in joy. Immediately he sells the house to him without saying another word as he also needs money for the operation of his mother. Srinivasan Iyengar goes house to change his residence in a hurry as he loves so much.

Vijay Kumar was haunted by the pain of being kicked out of his house even after the operation. Anyway, he wants to use Bharti as a bait to get back his house, and he wants to get back all the money he lost through her mother. Later that week, Vijay Kumar takes Bharti again to the guest house. Seeing Srinivasan Iyengar there, he says that "I come here every week for work", and introduces Bharti as his wife.

Srinivasan Iyengar also invites them to think that this is still your home.

Every week Vijay Kumar takes Bharti there, enjoys with her, takes money and goes back again, Bharti feels depressed inside when she realizes that Vijay Kumar is using her for money. When she is sitting on the sofa while listening her favourite song on TV at the same time, Srinivasan Iyengar is seen outside the house playing with birds among the forest trees.

After some days, the acquaintance between them turns into a bit of love. Bharti wants to tell him all the truth and start a new life with him.

Meanwhile, the day has come for Sulapani, who has been waiting for the opportunity since forever. Called Kadiresha and told him that "you have always been hoping for my daughter, today is the opportunity come home as soon as, and I will get my daughter ready".

Kadiresha was overjoyed with this, thinking it was a wonderful moment he had been waiting for a long time, and left as he was. Kadiresha, who takes five people with him wherever he goes, went alone this time. Kadiresha reached Sulapani's house with a bottle of alcohol as he went. Reaching Sulapani's house, Kadiresha couldn't stop her eagerness and asked her

"Where is your daughter? Send her quickly".

He noticed that the meaning of Sulapani's words which said that "you will be in heaven in a short time, why the patience is so fast?"

Kadiresha had come to that house many times, but this time something was different. Kadiresha, who felt it was not good to stay there for long, turned to leave when a small noise caught his attention.

Kadiresha's eyes narrowed in fear from a corner of the room and scanned the shadows that fell on the floor of the room. Looking at the shadow, Kadiresh realized that there was a third person in that room with them. Kadiresha staggered back a bit, because standing behind him was 'Michael', who was notorious for being a terrible rowdy on the streets. Kadiresha understands everything that is happening there and wants to save his life. Seeing the cruel grin on Michael's face, Sulapani heard stories of his brutality, but never expected to come face-to-face with the notorious rowdy sheeter in her own home.

With trembling hands, Kadiresha reached for the knife on the kitchen counter. But before Kadiresha could make any attempt to save himself, Michael rushed forward and grabbed him by the throat. His grip tightens with every passing second.

"Please, leave me", Kadiresha begged him while his tears streaming down on his face.

In a last act of desperation, Kadiresha reaches for a nearby candlestick and hits Michael hard on the head. Enraged, Michael took the axe he had brought with him and drove it hard into Kadiresha's heart with one blow. As Kadiresha's life is gasping for breath, Michael cuts his body more and more while looking at Sulapani.

The room fell silent as Michael stood over Kadiresha's lifeless body, the axe still smouldering in his hand. Sulapani's face lost colour when she saw the dire situation. Michael turned to Sulapani with a cold smile, his eyes glinting with malice, his gaze lingering over Sulapani's body parts.

"Looks like there's a little problem here, Sulapani," Michael said calmly, as if discussing the desire within him to Sulapani.

Sulapani thought that it would not be too difficult task to fulfil Michael's wish to escape from this cruel man. The whole house is filled with blood, Sulapani and Michael are drowning in lust with demon mentality next to the lifeless body of Kadiresha in that pool of blood that doesn't seem to have left the pain.

The next day

Kovalam Guest House,

Bharti, who is hoping for a new life, decides to tell Sulapani about her love no matter what and decides not to do such things from now on, and tells Vijay Kumar to leave her in home. Hearing all that, Vijay Kumar thinks that only one thing is running in his mind.

"Now Bharti has reversed like this, everything will be difficult to do, I will not get back what I have lost", he thinks it is impossible.

At the moment when he gently said, "Okay, will go", two police constables named 'Mambala' and 'Kunjappa' reached the guest house. Both of them are close friends of Vijay Kumar, and they all worked together in the same place earlier. Knowing that Vijay Kumar has come there, they also reach that guest house. After spending many days not together, they decide to have a good time drinking the wild liquor they brought with them. It is already night, Vijay Kumar sits to drink wild liquor with them, ignoring the Bharti request to drop her near the house.

As Bharti goes from there to Srinivasan, Mambala sees Bharti for the first time. He hopes to spend at least one night with her. Thinking that it is the right time, Vijay Kumar is drugged and drunk. While drunk, Mambala told Vijay Kumar about his wish, and Kunjappa asked him to give him a chance.

"Hope on the women shuts down all the thoughts in the mind. Does not even give time to think about good and bad. It doesn't really take into account whether it's right or wrong".

Unable to deny what his friends asked, Vijay Kumar goes downstairs, saying that he will take Bharti. Vijay Kumar takes Bharti's hand and pulls her back, who is already there to tell Srinivasan Iyengar everything that is on her mind. Vijay Kumar takes Bharti upstairs that he has to talk to you and tells Bharti that you should sleep with them both tonight and give them the comfort of bed.

Bharti doesn't agree with him and says that "I won't do anything like this again, I like Srinivasan, I want to live with him, and we both want to start a new life".

Vijay Kumar forces Bharti to sleep with both of them for this one night and from tomorrow live as her like. After a lot of arguments, Vijay Kumar pushed her into the room and stood outside at the entrance. Bharti stands her ground, refusing to succumb to Mambala and Kunjappa's outrageous actions. Bharti's heart pounded with fear and anger as two police officers advanced towards her with hateful eyes. She knew she had to think fast to escape this terrifying situation. Ignoring the fear that overwhelmed her, Bharti took a deep breath and prepared to do anything to save herself. Her eyes were fixed in defiance,

"I won't let you touch me", she declared firmly, though her voice was trembling.

However, she became a small rabbit between two pit foxes. Bharti realized that the foxes had overcome the power of the rabbit and started screaming loudly. Even so, with a small hope that Srinivasan Iyengar, who was in the room below, would come up and save her. The guest house, which had been peaceful until then, became violent with Bharti's screams. Hearing her cries, Srinivasan Iyengar comes running, thinking that she is in danger. But Vijay Kumar, who is waiting outside the door, stops him there and shouts that this is none of your business.

However, Srinivasan, who thinks Bharti's safety is important to him, gets into a heated argument with him. Unable to agree, he beats Vijay Kumar and enters. Seeing Bharti being attacked indiscriminately by the two, he could not bear it and tried to take her away from them. But in front of them are three, two together hold Srinivasan Iyengar tightly. Mambala, on the other hand, goes ahead with the aim of making Bharthi feel helpless. Realizing that she is helpless, breaks the wild liquor bottle next to Bharthi and commits suicide by stabbing herself.

Bharthi, who had given up everything for a life with Srinivasan Iyengar, even though she had done such things in the past, did not want to surrender to anyone but the one she loved, and finally left her life before Srinivasan Iyengar, whom she loved.

"Drunkenness will drive a man to any lengths, committing one mistake to another to get away from it".

Thinking that if someone find out about Bharti, they will lose their jobs, and they will have to go to jail as policemen, so they decide to kill Srinivasan Iyengar who is there to destroy the evidence.

While Srinivasan Iyengar, who was already seriously injured in their attack, ran away from them and went into the forest, three of them chased him and went into the same forest.

VII
CATCH THE CULPRIT

Sengaya Hut

Kovalanki Valley village

After Hearing all the story, Jeeva and Sneha asked Sengaya "what happened to Srinivasan Iyengar",

Sengaya says, "I don't know, but since then the three also stopped going to that guest house way. A few years later, Thangamani, who went that way to get honey, told the police that there was something in that house. The dead body has become a skeletal because of the passing of years".

Strangely, that same day night, someone also killed those two police constables Mambala and Kunjappa.

Vignesh Varma was listening to all this on the phone and cut the phone call, ignoring the fact that all the people of that village were making up stories. From there, Sneha and Jeeva, who turned back, reached the police quarters directly. Vignesh Varma and his team also reached there as the night was falling, and he sent his driver to his house, telling him to come early next day to go to Trivandrum.

Vignesh Varma was going through all the files of unexplained deaths that he had till then and found a case with the names of Mambala and Kunjappa in it. He assures them that they are really there, that the murders really happened, and that Sengaya's story is not a fabrication. As he took the case file and sat down at his desk, a thought crossed his mind. Don't know why what he heard in the phone call that evening echoed in Vignesh Varma's mind, as he had heard it somewhere before. But there is no chance because Vignesh Varma is telling himself that this is the first time he is coming to this town. He remembered everything he had heard in the phone call and started making notes one by one, hoping that it might be useful in the earlier investigation.

Every time he remembers, the only thing that haunts him is that he heard it somewhere before. If that single thought was burning Vignesh Varma, it would seep out of his brain like lava from a mountain of fire.

With wide-eyed surprise, Vignesh Varma immediately picks up the phone and says that everyone in his team should come here immediately, that we should go to Kovalanki valley now.

'Pratap' asked, sir but why at midnight?

Vignesh Varma replied him, because the voice I heard in the phone call in the evening and the voice in the voice recorder sent by Navya before her death, both are one and the same.

Shhhhh..... If you say........ You will die!

Vignesh Varma, who was in silence, was startled when he heard that voice so loudly. The voice he heard in that room created a little fear in his heart. He slowly goes to the room where Jeeva and Sneha are staying without even opening his mouth. He wakes both of them up saying come we have to leave here soon.

"What happened?

Where to at night? Where to go?" Says "Jeeva.

Instead, Vignesh Varma, without giving an answer, "silently come with me" and takes them both away.

Meanwhile, the power will be switched off. The three who suddenly went into the darkness took out their phones and put on flashlights and moved forward. Sinister shadows are creeping along the walls of the police quarters amidst the glare of those lights. As the night wore on, the shadows grew longer and the eerie silence of the police quarters was broken between three footsteps. It seems to the onlookers that the spirit has awakened to take revenge on them. Vignesh Varma gripped the torch tightly in his trembling hand. Suddenly, a loud noise echoed through the silence, and they all gasped in fear. Vignesh Varma's heart is pounding as he hears any other sounds in the dark. Just then, a shadowy figure emerged from the hallway, its form shrouded in darkness. Vignesh Varma's breath struck in his throat.

While trying to find out, Who is that? And what is it?

Vignesh, Jeeva and Sneha glance at each other as eerie laughter echoes in the dimly lit hall inside.

Laughter seemed to grow louder, taunting them from the shadows. Hearts pounding in their chests, Jeeva took a faltering step forward, his torch glancing across the hall like a beacon of hope in the darkness. But he could not see any trace of the person hiding in the shadows.

"Let's get out of here, I'm scared," Sneha says softly in her trembling voice.

Before Vignesh Varma and Jeeva could hear that, a cold breeze blew into the hall, extinguishing the flickering lights one by one.

As they reached the end of the hall, the laughter suddenly stopped. Vignesh Varma pushed the door open with trembling hands, and to those who were thinking of walking out of the open doors,

"Run away", the voice said loudly.

And without a moment's delay, the three of them went out, and the doors closed with a thud. The rest of them come running to the three of them, who are gasping for breath, saying that they got out safely.

At 6:10 AM,

Vignesh Varma takes everyone from the Kovalam Police and reaches Kovalanki Loya village. Within a moment of the hen's hatching, before the sun is even born, he goes around the whole village with his team. First he grabs Mariappa and takes him straight to Sengaya's hut.

Mariappa is outside the door of the hut, Vignesh Varma is behind him, team members are around the hut, and the policeman are around the village.

Vignesh Varma asks Mariappa to go and open the door. Everyone was ready with their guns in their hands, Mariappa went and opened the door slowly and saw that Sengaya was not there. No matter how hard he searched, he was not found, and they beat Mariappa and threatened him, "Tell me the truth about where he is or else you will be shot."

Mariappa replied, "I really don't know sir, I also saw him yesterday evening, he goes near the bank of the pond at this time every day. If he is there!"

From there they will reach near the bank of the pond which is half a kilometre away. The police cordoned around the pond, but they could not find a single person around the pond. Sengaya will come out of the water of that pond, steaming in the middle of the snowy smoke. When he saw the police in front of him.

"Sengaya, don't try to escape from here. Policemen are aiming guns at you around the pond. Even if you move your foot to the side, they will shoot you," warns Vignesh Varma.

Sengaya is arrested and taken to the police station, where he is beaten very severely without even a breather.

Vignesh Varma picked him up bleeding.

"Where is Rishi? Why did you kill Vishnu and Navya? Will you tell or die?" he insists.

Sengaya gets out of the confusion after a while but says,

"Who is the Rishi sir? Who is this Vishnu and Navya? Why did I kill them?"

Jeeva and Sneha reach there while Vignesh Varma is shouting at him to tell the truth without playing drama.

Hearing all that, both of them said, "Didn't we come to your hut yesterday evening, you told us everything that happened to Bharti in that guest house, Mariappa was also with us."

Sengaya says, who is this Bharti? I am seeing you for the first time.

Vignesh Varma gets angry and starts beating him again. Sengaya, who could not stand the blows, said, "I am telling the truth, sir, I have not been in the village since yesterday afternoon. If my health is not good, I went to the government hospital. If you want, ask the doctor there and find out, sir."

Vignesh Varma pauses for a moment and asks if what you said is a lie, you will die and calls the doctor's phone number, to which the doctor replies, "Yes, he was here till last night."

At once everyone there is surprised, the courage they had until then is turning into a bit of fear. Doubts are strong in the hearts, there is only one doubt on everyone's face.

Who was seen in that hut when we went with Mariappa? That's Jeeva, Sneha both said,

Who said everything I heard in the phone call yesterday evening? Vignesh Varma said,

To whom they were immersed in their own doubts. The only thought that shook them from the midst of those doubts was like - "Bharti?"

So in the midst of their worries, a phone call reaches them. While trying to find out what it is, they hear the words of the other person and suddenly leave the place and reach the edge of the forest towards the north of the Kovalam guest house. That place is the first part for those on the other side of the forest but the last part for Kovalam.

Someone called them and came towards them and said, "See if you are searching for this person, who is advertised in the newspaper", points to the fallen Rishi in the middle of the trees. Vignesh Varma tries to wake up Rishi who has fallen down, but he is not in consciousness and is rushed to the hospital. Vignesh Varma is there and starts interrogating the person who gave them the information.

He says, "My name is Rangi, I work here on a daily basis for this road work. I saw your advertisement in the newspaper in my village before I came. That is why I remember. I called you when I came here and saw that the trees were felled in the middle. I don't know what else to do."

Vignesh Varma gave him some money and from there reached the hospital and asked Rishi what happened when he came to conscious,

Rishi says, "I don't remember anything. I don't know what happened."

From there, he sends Rishi to home in Chennai with Jeevan and Sneha. Vignesh Varma, on the other hand, is determined to stay that night and finish the remaining work and leave. Tomorrow morning he takes the driver and reaches the registration head office in Trivandrum. Sometime 25 years ago, the documents were not yet computerized, so they had to come to the main office in Trivandrum instead of the sub- registrar's office for those documents. While giving all the details and turning over all the old documents there, a file related to the Kovalam Guest House is found. Vignesh Varma is surprised to see that the owner of the guest house is Vijay Kumar. Because according to what he heard in the phone call that day, he wrote the house to Srinivasan Iyengar, the documents should also bear his name, and he did not understand why Vijay Kumar's name was there. While taking all the details, Vignesh Varma greets the driver as he is seen his friend is working in the office.

"These are all very old documents, some of them have been computerized and some of them are still there", the registrar says, after looking at the details after knowing what they had come here for.

Vignesh Varma asks, "Can you please check and tell me what is wrong with this guest house documents?"

If he takes the details of those documents and checks them on the computer, Vijay Kumar's name is there too. But there is a pending application connected to it, open it and look at the details, it appears that once in 2017, a person has applied to change the guest house in his name. Vignesh Varma asks for the details of the person, and registrar says someone named Aditya.

Aditya? Vignesh says in surprise.

"Yes, his full name is 'Aditya Vijay Kumar'. He has applied to change the guest house documents from father to son. But he has not changed those documents so far, so it is still pending," says the registrar.

Hearing all that, Vignesh Varma becomes silent for a while.

"Is Aditya, Vijay Kumar's son?" After a long time, he recovered from that surprise and confirmed that it was the day before Mridula's death.

Mridula was murdered the next day and since then Aditya has been missing.

If Aditya did the murder and ran away, he might have changed all the documents and sold the guest house to someone in these 5 years.

But still they are in the name of Vijay Kumar which means he did not run away, surely Aditya also died in that house, but his dead body was destroyed by someone, cleverly thinking that the crime of murder was pushed on Aditya, Vignesh Varma takes his details in the application and goes away from there.

VIII
THE MYSTERY EXPLANATION

Next Day

The Journal Office

Hyderabad, Telangana

The Journal is a leading company that brings out the hidden truths through different types of research and publishes them to know the entire population of the country. Vignesh Varma reaches that office directly with the details he has collected about Aditya.

When asked about Aditya there, "He is my friend, but from some years he did not come here, and the policemen said that he killed and ran away," says 'Shiva Reddy'.

He says, "I'm Vignesh Varma, the policeman who is handling the case, can you tell me everything about Aditya." Shiva Reddy starts saying this.

Aditya and I studied at the same time and joined the same job. What we do here is to write and publish articles so that everyone knows the truths and mysteries that no one knows, no one can know, and the forgotten truths and mysteries are known with great difficulty. Aditya loved this job so much that he worked harder than all of us. The quest to know is so great for him that it is because of that quest that he once found mystery about a skeleton somewhere in a forest in Kerala some 20 years back, and it went into unsolved cases. He told me the day before that he was going to that place with some things he knew to gather full details about it, That is when the last time I saw him. A few days later, the police came and said that he killed Mridula and fled. But they both fell in love and the marriage was also fixed, so why does Aditya kill Mridula?

Isn't Vijay Kumar is father of Aditya?

Where is he now?

Vignesh Varma takes the address of their house. And reaches Aditya's house in Kachiguda and meets Vijay Kumar. "You may not know me, but I know you very well. You worked as forest ranger in Kovalam and later got transferred to another place and took VRS and settled in Hyderabad. I did not come here for that reason.

But do you know that why your son went to those Kovalam forests? Or

Did he leave unknowingly?

Because no one knows about that forest better than you," says Vignesh Varma.

Vijay Kumar - "After looking at the files with Aditya, I came to know that he found one guest house mystery in that forest. Even though I told him not to go, he didn't listen to me.

A heated argument took place between the two of us, and in that order, I said that the guest house was ours, but we left it and came here. I told him that it is not good to go there now as it is a danger to life. Later he listened to me and said he doesn't go there, but he left with a message that he will come back to take possession of that guest house when we see him in the morning. Some days after, the policeman said he killed Mridula and ran away".

You hid the truth from your son. Do you know the cost of the lie you told that day? That is your son's life.

Don't understand? Let me tell you clearly.

"Aditya had a fight with you on the evening of 26th January,

On the morning of 27th he reached Thiruvananthapuram along with the girl he loved, Mridhula.

And there he applied for the change of guest house documents at the head registration office that day.

In the evening they both went to a hotel and the next day early, i.e. 28th afternoon, they both approached the guest house. Due to heavy rain that day, they had to spend the night in that guest house. At that time, he found something he wanted in that house, he took it, the next day the forest officers found Mridula's body there, but Aditya was nowhere to be found.

They registered an FIR saying that he had killed and fled, and they came to you for investigation. Another thing is that your two friends Mambala and Kunjappa were also killed that same night. I don't think that your son has returned home after that day and that he is still alive. Surely your son was also killed along with Mridula that night".

Vijay Kumar asks Vignesh Varma, who is getting up and leaving

"Who killed my son?"

"Didn't I tell you before, the cost of that lie you told to your son about your past is his life. The mistake you made in that guest house cost your son.

Mambala, Kunjappa, Aditya, these three were killed by only one.

And that one is the man you three were killed together.

If you don't remember the past, just try to remember it, if you remember it, take appropriate precautions. For I do not think that the death that has come to them will not come to you," he warns.

Vignesh Varma's words caused fear in Vijay Kumar's eyes, and got a name from his thoughts - Bharti?

"Yes". He says and leaves from there.

From there, Vignesh Varma, who reached Kovalam, gives all the details and evidence related to the case to the Kovalam police and closes Aditya's case. After reaching his elder sister's house in Chennai, he tells everything that happened, he wants to wake up early tomorrow morning, and told her sister that we are going to Nagercoil, he eats and goes to his room to go to sleep, he stops by Rishi's room in the middle. Talking to him for a while and instilling courage in him, on his way back he sees an old camera there.

He asks Rishi "where you got such an old camera?"

To which Rishi says, "I found it in that guest house".

Vignesh Varma looked at Rishi in shock and remembered what Mariappa had said to them that day in his mind.

"It is a cursed place, and if anyone goes there alone, and touches the things there, they will die."

Vignesh Varma, afraid that if Rishi brings the camera home with him, she will definitely not leave it, so Vignesh Varma sleeps with Rishi that night.

After waking up in the morning, while Vignesh Varma is leaving to go to Nagercoil, Rishi's mother brings a dream catcher in his room so that the dream he had the other day does not come again. When Rishi suspiciously asks what dream he had, she says it was last night.

Meanwhile, Jeeva and Sneha reach there and understand what happened and told him their dream about what happened in that guest house before, and they tell that Vishnu and Navya died because of that. Rishi, on the other hand, is deeply saddened to know about the death of his friends and says that he never had such a dream that night.

Friends ask why you went to the forest, after looking here and there in the wind.

"Why did I go to the forest?

I got up that night and went downstairs for water, and then I opened my eyes and found myself in the hospital, not knowing what happened," says Rishi.

Vignesh Varma, listening to everything Rishi said, wonders why he went to that place without his knowledge. Meanwhile, he got a phone call from Kovalam Police. Vignesh Varma says his wife leave the luggage in house, I have to go now to Kovalam not Nagercoil.

When he reached there, the Kovalam police showed him a skeleton and told him that it was found during the road works in the north of the Kovalam forest. Strangely, Rangi said that this skeleton was found while removing the trees where the Rishi was found, and on examination, it was found to be a person who died almost 25 years ago.

Recalls that word In a phone call to Vignesh Varma that evening, Bharti, in the form of Sengaya, that the three of them chased the injured Srinivasan Iyengar into the forest.

If he looks at the lab reports with suspicion, Doctor mentioned that it is a man's skeleton and broken bones, which means that someone attacked him and killed him. Vignesh Varma's suspicion turns into a slightly stronger belief. Determines that the skeleton is Srinivasan Iyengar.

When Rishi was coming from the trip, brought the Srinivasan Iyengar camera home with him. And Rishi did not have the dream of the other four, but that night he came to this forest unknowingly and fell at the place where Srinivasan Iyengar was killed. It all seems like a pre-arranged plan to Vignesh Varma, who is thinking about what happened in the guest house, the whereabouts of Rishi only after that night when we left here, and since then all the deaths have been revealed one by one, and finally today the skeleton of Srinivasan Iyengar was found in the road works.

But who planned it?

All the questions that have been left for so many days have been answered today. But who has done all this to know all these truths?

IX
THE DEMON REVENGE

Warning of Death

Vignesh Varma, who was scratching his hair with crazy questions, got only one answer - Bharti.

Bharti's revenge that haunts everyone finally reveals the truth behind her death. It is clear that she has been wronged by Vijay Kumar, who has been on the run for years. Vijay Kumar's nefarious deeds are narrated by Vignesh Varma. Vignesh Varma realizes Bharti's revenge that Vijay Kumar who lost his son will definitely come there.

Immediately, Vignesh Varma calls to Vijay Kumar, but his phone does not work. He calls Shiva Reddy who is staying there and tell him make Vijay Kumar to talk to me. Siva Reddy reached there after a long time and called Vignesh Varma again and said that Vijay Kumar is not here, his wife said that he had gone somewhere yesterday evening. Sensing the situation, Vignesh Varma reached the guest house with the police, and there Sengaya is seen using all the evil lessons he has learned so far and provoking Bharti. Sengaya's actions are at peak's level and Vignesh Varma stops him. Sengaya telling him to leave me, I have to end this devil somehow, but Vignesh Varma doesn't care.

And asks him back, what are you doing here?

Why did you come here? What do you need?

"I need it, because this devil killed my brother," says Sengaya.

Did this devil kill your brother? Vignesh Varma asks who your brother is.

And Sengaya replied 'Thangamani'.

Vignesh Varma asked who this Thangamani was, and he said, "Whoever opened the doors of this guest house that day, because of whomever this demon came out and killed everyone from that day, it is because of my brother Thangamani, a honey seller". Sengaya says that this demon killed him.

Is that honey seller your brother? Vignesh Varma says in surprise.

Yes, I went to the forest along with my brother for honey as there was a big demand that day. On our way back, it was raining heavily, and we came near this guest house. He said that he had noticed many times the sound of songs coming from inside, he was afraid to look through the latch of the door to see who was inside and brought me from there. I begged my brother not to tell anyone, but he did not listen and told the police, they broke the door and took the skeleton away. This ghost killed the two constables Mambala and Kunjappa who came for investigation that night. Since then, I have been guarding my brother carefully out of fear, but within a few days this demon killed my brother too. Even to this day, I have not forgotten that hell when he was bleeding and dying at my feet. That's why I have worked so hard since then, I have come back somewhere, learn all these lessons with someone and finish it, says Sengaya.

Meanwhile, the coolness of the forest is palpable in the air. Shadows dance between the trees, and the night seems to breathe. On a moonless night, the Kovalanki valley village on the edge of the forest was besieged by loud cries. All the villagers tremble in fear as rumours spread that an evil ghost is haunting their land, causing desperation among all. Sengaya cannot escape from Vignesh Varma in a guest house in the centre of Kovalam forests, shrouded in thick fog. Vijay Kumar reaches that guest house along with 'Marthanda Kurivi' to give strength to Sengaya. Marthanda Kurivi is a famous experienced great wizard with transcendental and tantric knowledge. All of them came together to face the demon that took their lives and take revenge. Vignesh Varma got that Vijay Kumar has made a deal with dark forces that he cannot fathom. Vignesh Varma and the Kovalam Police who are with him realize that it will be a tough task for them to face them.

Blocked all the sides of guest house and creates a huge bonfire and starts trying to trap Bharti in it.

Bharti's soul realizes with the most powerful great light, unending passion, breaking the fetters of anger. Undeterred by the monstrous appearance of the ghost, Sengaya and Marthanda Kurivi stood firm. But the demon, fuelled by decades of grief and rage, resists their efforts, its cries echoing through the forest like mournful wails. But in order to control the tremors of the demon, Marthanda Kurivi took out his talisman and held it up to reflect the moonlight. As the demon retreated from the bright light coming from the talisman, Sengaya and Marthanda Kurivi seized the opportunity to execute their plan. Accelerate their mantras and make the demon sit in the burning furnace. While the flames are rising all around, Bharti in the middle is getting angry. Meanwhile, Sengaya, with the talisman's lights, traps the demon in the dark shadows within it.

As the demon was subdued, its screams that haunted the forest faded into silence. Vijay Kumar jumps with joy as Sengaya and Marthanda Kurivi fulfil his goal. We must pass this forest before the first light of the sun falls in the sky.

Marthanda says "that this forest demon has the most strength, we should leave this guest house, this forest as soon as possible.

Dark forces lurk in every tree in this forest, which can attack us at any moment. Even though this journey is very dangerous, we must overcome it at all costs."

They packed all their things and started their journey, holding the talisman tightly in their hands. Shadows danced across the walls as the very foundations of the guest house shook at the intensity of the supernatural battle. Their footsteps echoed through the trees. They are ready to face the challenges that come their way.

Vignesh Varma and the Kovalam Police are chasing them. The roots of the trees are reaching out from their soil and trying to stop them. While they are moving ahead, avoiding all of them, Vijay Kumar gets stuck in the tree roots. In order to escape him, the talisman in Sengaya's hand slips and falls down and breaks. Soon the ghost comes out of it and reaches the guest house before opening its eyelids with a terrible laugh.

"It is very dangerous to go to that guest house again, now the revenge of that demon will reach the level of peaks, besides this all this forest will be united, if we go there, our lives will be lost in the air," Marthanda Kurivi said.

No matter what he said, Vijay Kumar forced them all again with a grudge against Bharti. He takes both to there.

Like adding fuel to the fire, Vijay Kumar, who had brought them there again, was thrown against the wall with one shot and broke his back. The shadows of the guest house danced like an audience in the moonlight, and the air grew thick with the stench of decay. Suddenly, Bharti emerges from that darkness, like Lord Kaleshwar, with fiery eyes burning brighten. Sengaya and Marthanda Kurivi were casting the most powerful spells they knew. However, their efforts only fuelled the demon's vengeful wrath. Aiming to destroy everyone there, it tortures and tortures and kills each one. While everyone there is getting stronger like sacrificial animals to her anger, Bharti is finally approaching Vignesh Varma in the same vengeful flame when she hears someone step inside.

Bharti sees Rishi with a camera in his hand, looking away with burning anger. He raises both his hands and tries to give the camera to Bharti. Seeing that, Bharti calmed down and felt sad that he was going to kill those who had helped him.

In the climactic struggle between light and shadow, Bharti's soul longs to find peace in the embrace of eternal night after all the terrible conflict between men and spirit.

Bharti's eyes filled with joy when she saw Rishi's mother, who had followed in search of her son.

Bharti Fondly called her 'Zoya'

Knowing that Rishi is her son, Bharti returns the camera to Rishi and merges into that darkness forever. All the trees there breathed in peace, and the stars in the sky began to shine with a new radiance.

Vignesh Varma leaves the guest house with all of them, not understanding why Bharti called them Zoya when Rishi's mother's name is Kalpana.

"The problem they faced has now been solved. But, echoes of supernatural powers are always move in the air."